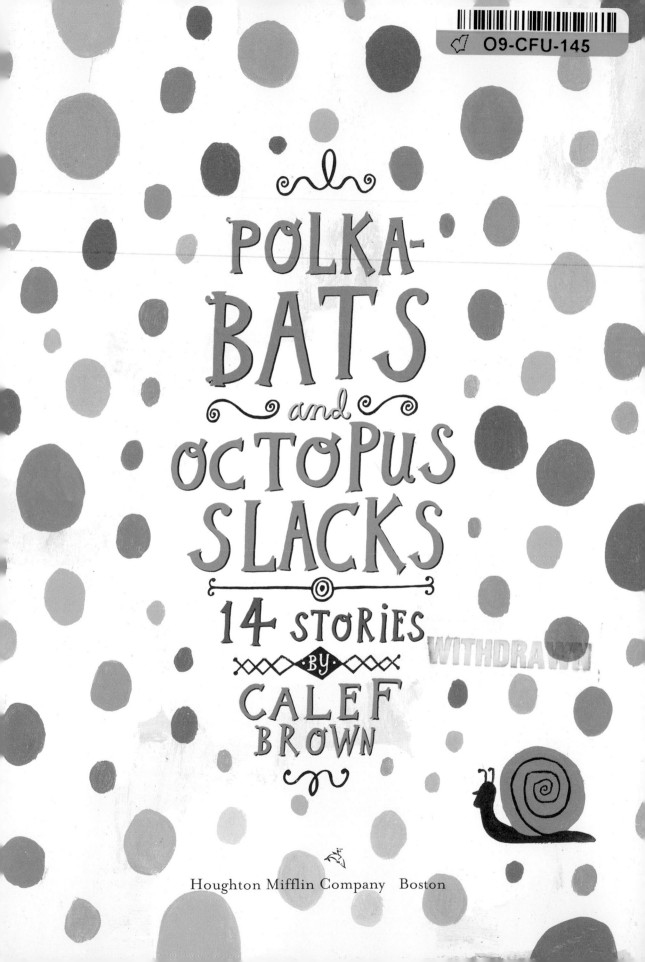

POLKA-BATS AND OCTOPUS SLACKS

14 STORIES BY CALEF BROWN

O9-CFU-145

WITHDRAWN

Houghton Mifflin Company   Boston

T 162248

VISTA GRANDE
PUBLIC LIBRARY

for KatyNickEmilyHannahClaireMollyandAlex!

Polkabats and Octopus Slacks
14 Stories
by Calef Brown

Art Direction: Calef Brown, George Mimnaugh
Design: George Mimnaugh

Copyright © 1998 by Calef Brown

All rights reserved. For information about permission to reproduce selections from this book, write to Permissions, Houghton Mifflin Company, 215 Park Avenue South, New York, New York 10003.

The text of this book is set in Emigre™, Mrs Eaves Roman.

Library of Congress Cataloging-in-Publication Data

Brown, Calef.
Polkabats and Octopus Slacks: 14 stories / by Calef Brown, [author and illustrator].
p.   cm.
Summary: Fourteen rhyming tales about a variety of fanciful topics.
RNF ISBN 0-395-85403-2   PAP ISBN 0-618-11129-8
[1. Stories in rhyme.] I. Title.
PZ8.3.B8135Sn   1998
[Fic]-dc21   97-12011 CIP AC

PAP ISBN-13: 978-0618-11129-9

Manufactured in the United States of America

WOZ 10 9 8 7 6

14 STORIES

Kansas City Octopus

Kansas City Octopus

is wearing fancy slacks.

Bell-bottom,

just got 'em,

fifty bucks including tax.

Red corduroy,

and boy-o-boy,

they fit like apple pie.

Multi-pocket snazzy trousers

custom made for octopi.

Fantastic plastic stretch elastic

keeps 'em nice and tight.

Kansas City Octopus

is looking good tonight!

HighwiRE 66

Another tightrope traffic jam

on Highwire 66.

Fifty thousand acrobats

rehearsing fancy tricks.

The problem started down the wire,

some clown sat down to change a tire.

It took some time to get it fixed

on busy Highwire 66.

Ed

Introducing Ed

with cherries on his head.

He says "I like the color,"

so all his stuff is red.

Last week he had a fever,

his head was very warm,

Ed smelled like cherry marmalade

and flies began to swarm.

Funky Snowman

Funky Snowman loves to dance.

You'd think he wouldn't have much chance

without two legs

or even pants.

Does that stop Funky Snowman?

No!!

Turn up the music with the disco beat,

when you're in the groove, you don't need feet.

Crowds come out and fill the street.

Kick it, Funky Snowman!!

Snails

It never fails, those pesky snails
are always in the pudding.
Lousy guests, those nasty pests,
they're always up to something.

I've tried like mad to find their nest
but snails are smart I must confess.
The trails they leave can fool the best,
and snails are good at hiding.

Oh well, at least they don't make threats,
they don't eat meat,
they don't place bets,
they almost always pay their debts
and never puff on cigarettes.
I think I'll keep those snails as pets
and feed them lots of pudding.

POLKABATS

The Polkabats are on the loose,
a flapping flock of flying fury.
All the spotted bats are out
(except the ones on jury duty).

Loudly screeching nasty words
like "Stroganoff"
to scare the birds
while dropping smelly polka-turds
on people down below.

the Bathtub Driver

The Bathtub Driver is coming to town

with imported shampoo

that he sells by the pound.

His one-legged duck

rides along for good luck

yelling "Three for a buck!"

when they're having a sale.

The Bathtub Driver won't stay very long,

his supply of shampoo will soon be all gone.

So get up and sing out a fabulous song

for a sweet-smelling,

soap-selling,

tub dwelling guy

and his one-legged duck named Alphonso.

SKELETON FLOWERS

Late October showers

bring delicate skeleton flowers.

A ghostly sight

on Halloween night,

they softly glow for hours.

CLEMENTOWN

Clementown is greenish,

the people tall and leanish,

the dogs bark very loudish,

but not because they're meanish.

The food is rather reddish,

delicious radish relish,

there's never any rubbish,

that would just be foolish.

the LONELY SURFER

In a dry and dusty desert town

the lonely surfer hangs around.

Perched upon a prickly pear,

he usually wears a worried frown.

People ask the surfer dude,

"Why so far from the ocean blue?"

"Because I'm so afraid of sharks,"

he says, "and water too!"

MULLIGAN POKER

Fido and Rover play Mulligan Poker,

a most ridiculous game.

The only rule is to act like a fool

and pretend all the cards are the same.

The game has begun

when the winner has won

and the loser is wearing a smile.

Then it starts over

so Fido and Rover

can chew on the cards for a while.

Georgie Spider

Georgie Spider catches flies

but never eats the little guys.

Instead he cooks up insect pies.

He doesn't use the legs or eyes

or any artificial dyes.

They're very good

(though small in size).

At last year's fair they won first prize.

So if you're hungry, stop on by,

give Georgie's fresh fly pie a try!

ELIZA'S JACKET

Eliza has a jacket,

a jacket made of pockets.

The pockets all have numbers,

numbers on the jacket pockets.

Pocket three has bees inside,

sixteen contains their honey.

Number eight has cracker crumbs

and wads of Turkish money.

Twenty-three is filled with gum

(all unchewed I hope),

while right next door in twenty-four

is kept a one-inch piece of rope.

Thirteen is packed with useless facts,

and four has melted snow.

What's in the rest

you'll have to guess.

It's not for us to know.

SLEEPING FRUIT

Dozing daily

Sleeping fruit

Napping nightly

Sleeping fruit

Swaying slightly

Snoozing soundly

Snoring softly

Sleeping fruit